Princess Sara

written and illustrated
by Rebecca Bell

dr. ball

Bouncing Ball Books
"From the Florida Swamp to Readers Everywhere"

Princess Sara
Rebecca Bell

Copyright© 2000 by Bouncing Ball Books

Library of Congress
ISBN 80-902746-8-4
EAN 978-80-902746-8-6

TXu1-206-630 2004

printed in Czech Republic

www.bouncingballbooks.com

1

Once upon a time there lived
of a far away land. Her name
her Princess Sara.

Princess Sara lived in a larg
He was going to grow up to be
had almost everything that

oung girl. She was a Princess
was Sara. Everybody called

castle. She had a big brother.
King. That's nice. Princess Sara
she wanted.

3

Princess Sara was usually
would stand in front of her mirror
Her mirror did not tell her

She knew that she was
not the cook. She was not
Sara wanted to know what she

happy. But sometimes she
and wonder, "Who am I?"
who she was.

not the gardener. She was
the housekeeper. Princess
would be when she grew up.

Princess Sara asked her
when I grow up ?" Sara's
" Why, any thing you so desire."

mother, the Queen, said, "Well,
from a far away land and
always said that. Her brother,
always be my little sister," Never

family, "What should I be
father, the King, told her,
He always said that. Sara's

you will marry a Prince
live happily ever after." She
the Prince said, " You will
mind that.

Princess Sara liked what the
the problem. She didn't know wha
morning thinking about what she so

So Princess Sara went to
cheer herself up. She put on her
found her flower basket and went

King said most. But that was
she so desired. She spent all
desired. But she still didn't know.

pick flowers in the garden to
blue dress and mocassins,
out side. She loved flowers.

Princess Sara walked all the
starting to go down. She had
flowers but still wondered "Who

Then she heard someone
tree and waited quietly. The
looked kind and gentle. He

way to the lake. The sun was
a basketful of beautiful
am I?"

talking. She hid behind a
young man and his horse
also had baskets of something.

Princess Sara's father
to the young man. Sara stood up
this land?" The young man was
was on my way to the monastery,
said, "Oh, really? And what is your nam

The young man answered, "yes,
not poor, but I am lost. Would
the monastery, if you please. And
name?" Princess Sara said, "Zenc
direct you to the monastery. Bu

owned the land. She decided to talk
and asked, "What are you doing on
surprised and said, "Oh, me? I
but I got lost." Princess Sara
you poor lost soul?"

eally. And my name is Zeno. I am
you be so kind as to direct me to
flower girl in blue, what is your
my name is Sara and I can
I have a few questions..."

Sara asked, " What is in you
Why are you going to the monastery
you walked up?" Zeno said, "Oh, m
stallion. René meet Sara, flower girl."
knew he was meeting <u>Princess</u> Sara
Princess always wears a blue dress and

Zeno continued, "I come from a land
my baskets that I picked along the w
monastery, the monks have some book
the raspberries as a gift." And Sara

baskets? Where do you come from?
And who were you talking to when
horse. Sara, meet René, my white
René bowed his head in honor. René
because city horses said, "The
mocassins while picking flowers."

far away. I have raspberries in
for the monks. When I get to the
for me to read and I will give them
said, "Really?" And Zeno said, "Really".

Sara said, "Oh. Well, the
from here. Follow the lake that
clearing, look up the hill." Zena
more. Those sure are pretty flowers
"Oh, no," said Princess Sara, "The
some with you." "Thank you,"
of my raspberries." Sara and

monastery is about an hour walk

way and when you get to the

said, "OK, I don't feel lost any

Do you sell them in the market?"

are for my room. Please take

said Zeno, "And please take some

Zeno exchanged gifts.

"I have to keep going,"
on the path. "OK, bye." "OK,
Zeno walked away from each

Every few minutes, Zeno
the flowers Sara had given
Sara would eat a raspberry
Sara was wishing that Zeno
they could get married and

said Zeno. He started walking
bye." And Princess Sara and
other.

would lean over and smell

him. Every few minutes,
Zeno had given her. Princess
was a Prince. Then, maybe,
live happily ever after.

As Princess Sara walked back to
she so desired. Maybe her father and
she would always be a Princess. Mayb
a Prince from a far away land.

Zeno was a hard worker. He picke
He talks to his horse. Zeno was kind
has a good mind. He reads books.
She wished that he was a Prince
was not watching the path as

he castle, she thought about what
mother and brother were right. Maybe
she would live happily ever after with
Princess Sara thought about Zeno.

ll those raspberries. Zeno was gentle.
e brings gifts to the monastery. Zeno
Princess Sara was thinking about Zeno,
from a far away land. Princess Sara
she wondered toward the waterfall.

Princess Sara's mocassin got
She went tumbling down the
out one word, "ZENO", with all

Now Zeno and René were almos
tweeked back and Zeno thought
wind. Zeno remembered Sara.
herself and it was almost
could happen. Sara might be
my help."

caught in a strong wild vine.
hill. As she fell, she called
her might.

out of the woods. René's ears
e heard his name called in the
She was walking home all by
dark. He thought, "Anything
in trouble. Sara might need

Zeno did not wait one more second.
He quickly threw battle shirts over
unwrapped his sword and helmet.
"René, gallop!" René galloped

As René galloped, Zer
being brave. Prince Zeno didn't rea
Prince Zeno sometimes wondered i
father in the far away land.

He put the baskets on the ground.
himself and René. Then Zeno
He mounted René and said,
back along the path through the woods.

thought about courage and
like to kill dragons or fight in wars,
he would be a good King like his

Rene' and Prince Zeno stopped
Zeno saw Sara's mocassin caught
down the hill and saw Sara at
second. He commanded, "Down
your hooves." And down they went,

Prince Zeno knelt over Sara
whispered in her ear, "Wake up my
raspberry boy. Sara wake up now,
Prince Zeno dropped raspberry juice

n the path by the lake. Prince
in the wild vine. Then he looked
the bottom. Zeno did not wait a
the hill René, as if wings were on
bumping and sliding.

on the ground. "Sara, Sara," Zeno
lovely flower girl. It is Zeno, your
sweet flower, and taste the berry."
onto her pale lips.

Prince Zeno waited and Princess
a young Prince. On his rest was
She knew that he was the Prince of the

René picked up the flower basket
was Princess Sara's family symbo
that she was Princess of the Cast
Prince Zeno looked at each other.

Sara blinked. She saw a man,
his family symbol and shoulder badge.
ar Away Land.

cloth with his teeth. On the cloth
and badge. Prince Zeno knew
By The Lake. Princess Sara and
They both smiled.

Princess Sara and Prince Zeno
after season they took long walks
Sometimes they would sit by the fire
that the monks gave them. When the
and the flowers bloomed again,
still walking and talking. And now

Sara didn't worry
too much any more. And Zeno
and courageous. One day at
Sara to the place where they

became very good friends . Season
together by the lake and talked.
and be very quiet and read the books
raspberries were ripe the next year
Princess Sara and Prince Zeno were
they were a little more grown up.

about   what she so desired
didn't wonder if he was brave
sunset, Prince Zeno brought Princess
had met.

Prince Zeno had a special present shirt. It was blue and had a symbol was the sun setting over castle in the land far away. Princes Zeno?" Prince Zeno said, "It is and my family put together, Sara."

"Zeno, what are you saying?" asked married and live happily ever after," "Really," said Zeno. And Sara

for René. It was a new parade
beautiful new symbol on it. The
the hills by the lake and the
Sara said, "What does this mean,
the new symbol of your family
Sara's face became happy.

Sara. "I think that we could get
said Zeno. "Really?" said Sara.
said, "Me too."

It took a whole year to prepare
and Prince Zeno. But the waiting
people from both lands had a

And Princess Sara
Lived Happily

for the wedding of Princess Sara
was worth it because all of the
very good time.

And Prince Zeno
Ever After.

The End